DYBBUK

DYBBUK

A Version

by BARBARA ROGASKY

illustrated by

LEONARD EVERETT FISHER

Holiday House / New York

Special thanks to Rabbi Leonard A. Schoolman,
Director of the Center for Religious Inquiry
in New York City, for his assistance

The text typeface is Weiss.
The artist created the illustrations
using acrylic paints on #80 Bainbridge board.
www.holidayhouse.com
First Edition
1 3 5 7 9 10 8 6 4 2

Library of Congress Cataloging-in-Publication Data

Rogasky, Barbara.
Dybbuk : a version / by Barbara Rogasky ;
pictures by Leonard Everett Fisher.— 1st ed.
p. cm.
Summary: In this retelling of a Jewish legend, a girl is possessed
by the spirit of the man she was destined to, but did not, marry.
ISBN 0-8234-1616-X (hardcover)
[1. Jews—Europe—Folklore. 2. Folklore—Europe.]
I. Fisher, Leonard Everett, ill. II. Title.
PZ8.1.R65Dy 2005
398.2'089'924—dc22
2004060624

ISBN-13: 978-0-8234-1616-5
ISBN-10: 0-8234-1616-X

In loving memory,

for Harry and Rebecca Rubin,

my *zayde* and *bubbe*

B. R.

To John and Kate

L. E. F.

CONTENTS

I have to tell this story in my own way.

It is a complicated story,

and I will try to make it as simple as I can.

It happened a very long time ago.

Some say it could not have happened at all, but I think it could have.

There are those who think it is a sad tale,

meant to frighten young and old and to teach them a lesson.

Exactly what that lesson is, I'm not sure about myself.

PART I

Many many years ago, there was a tiny village called Brinitz. Only Jews lived there, most of them very religious. They met with non-Jews only on market day, and only when they had to. No love was lost between them, believe me.

The synagogue in Brinitz was very old, so old no one knew the length of its years. Its few rooms were small and dark, its walls dark too—and damp, some said, with the tears of Jews. The one bright spot was the Holy Ark, where the scrolls of the Torah were held. The cloth that covered them was rich in color and design, the silver breastplate deeply and elaborately carved. The wooden doors, kept open much of the time, were themselves burnished with age. The eternal light hanging above the Ark made all seem to glow.

The synagogue was almost never empty. Several men spent every day there. They remained to study, or so they said, and to say prayers for those who asked, if any did. For a few pennies—what more could most villagers afford?—they would pray for luck, for health, a safe journey, to remove the evil eye. Enough prayers, enough pennies, and they would have a little wine or brandy. Then their prayers took the form of wordless melody and dance, all in joy to the great glory of the Master of the Universe.

Pious and sincere they were. But how long could they keep their noses in books, and could they pray all the time? This day, they were talking among themselves. Gossip is a sin, but maybe not such a big one all the time.

"So tell me already, what does he want?"

One of them, half dozing, sat up at this. "Who? Who wants what?"

"Who? The richest man in Brinitz, that's who."

"Ah, Sender."

"Yes, Sender."

"Nu? So what's happening?"

"He tries to arrange a marriage for his Leah, his beauty of a daughter, and—"

"That's bad?"

"No, no! What, I'm not a Jew? But he wants—"

"So say it already!"

"He wants a rich man. And—"

"That's not good?"

"Oy, listen and you'll know."

"The family has to be rich, richer than Sender even. Sender demands—"

"I can just imagine."

"Believe you me, you can't imagine. Sender demands—"

"As if he didn't have enough money to take care of all Brinitz already!"

"Stop! Envy is a sin."

"One cannot hope for the blessings another has?"

"Listen, listen. That's not all Sender wants."

"So what else?"

"The groom must be so learned that—"

"Eh, a genius he wants."

"And more yet! The family has to agree to board Leah and the groom for five years."

"Five you heard? More. Not five. Ten!"

"Ten years? Whoever heard of such a thing? I tell you—"

"And why not? This way everyone gets something. The groom's family gets a pearl in Leah. And Leah can live proudly and have a life of silks and ease. God forbid a poor man should want her."

"No, no. Sender wants too much. I hear—"

"I hear he could not reach an agreement yet again."

"Yes. I hear too that he comes back to Brinitz today. With nothing."

"A surprise it's not. So he has found no one yet."

"Not yet. So, we shall see, we shall see. . . ."

It is time to tell you about Konin.

Konin was a poor orphaned scholar who lived only to learn. He traveled from town to town. Sometimes a peasant or another Jew would take him in his wagon for a while. But mostly he walked. And he studied. He studied each day and most of each night, read books even as he walked. Where did he sleep, how did he eat? When he came to a town, sometimes he would sleep on a bench in the synagogue. His stomach might know only a piece of stale bread or a bite of dry cheese. But mostly he depended on the charity of villagers and others to feed him and sometimes even to house him. After a few days, wherever he was, he would move on.

But not in Brinitz. He lingered in Brinitz. Why? Because of Leah.

And now it is time to tell you about Leah.

Leah was Sender's daughter, yes, quiet and beautiful. Pious and sweet natured. Goodness radiated from her almost like some light from within. Motherless—her mother died, may she know peace, giving birth to her. She was brought up by Fradeh, a virtuous woman orphaned from a poor family whom Sender took into his home to raise his daughter. When the time came, Leah would be a wonderful wife to a wonderful man, a jewel added to his family.

But Sender did not make this easy. Matchmakers sought him out left and right, each telling him about possible bridegrooms for Leah—naturally all were described as brilliant, handsome, and from a wealthy family—and each time Sender could not reach an agreement. He asked too much. Or perhaps

13

the heavens had a reason that Sender could not yet see. He would find out, but maybe not soon enough.

And here is where the story really begins.

Sender had asked Konin for the Sabbath meal—a good deed, and an easy one for Sender. Leah and Konin sat opposite each other.

Well, they knew. The minute Konin and Leah looked at each other, they knew. What did they know? They knew that they loved each other. More, they knew they were destined to be together. Such things happen.

His stomach full after the rich and delicious meal, Sender fell asleep for a moment.

Softly, Konin said to Leah, "I have known you all my life."

She replied, "Always."

With a snort, Sender awoke. "Nu," he said to Konin, "so tell me a little about you. Your family?"

"My mother, blessings be upon her, died giving birth to me. My father, may he know peace, died soon after."

Sender shook his head. "Oy, a pity, a pity. So, go on, go on."

"He was a learned man, kind and generous, I am told. A great loss to all. His name was Nisson."

Sender leaned forward on hearing this. "Nisson? Your father's name was Nisson?"

"Yes."

"Once I had a much-loved friend whose name also was Nisson." Sender fell silent for a moment, lost in memory. And this is what he remembered.

Nisson and Sender grew up together. They played together as children, they learned Hebrew and studied together, they even married the same week. Truly, they loved each other as close friends can.

Nisson moved away from Brinitz. But before he left, he and Sender made

a solemn pact. If one of their wives gave birth to a boy and the other to a girl, the children would be married when the time came.

They declared their pact during the High Holy Days, the time of the New Year and the most solemn and holy of all days. Their promise to each other was heard in heaven. It was not to be broken.

Years passed. Sender heard nothing from Nisson. Maybe he wondered why, but he was so busy getting rich that soon he gave it no thought. The pact with Nisson faded from his memory. But memory makes its own rules, and Konin's words brought the memory back to him. He pushed it away into forgetfulness again, for the results of doing otherwise were not bearable to him.

He should not have done that. Do you doubt it?

Now, Sender was not a fool. He noticed the veiled looks that passed between Konin and Leah, he felt the weight of their silences. This connection could not be. He spoke up.

"You have heard what I seek for my Leah?"

Startled, Konin nodded. "Yes, Reb Sender."

"Ai, I tell you, Konin, it is hard, very hard, to find the right match for her."

Konin's words stumbled out. "Ah, yes, she is, um, she is, ah, a true beauty, Reb Sender."

Leah blushed, as uncomfortable as Konin. She excused herself from the table.

Sender went on. "Beauty? She is more than beautiful. She has all the virtues of a good Jewish daughter. She has them ten times over."

"Reb Sender,"—Konin's voice was low and tense—"Reb Sender, I would like—if you—if it is possible—would she—can she—"

Sender interrupted. "She deserves the best, the very best. She must never want for a thing, not a single thing. Do you wonder I seek wealth for her?" He shook his head. "No no, a poor man she can never marry. Never."

Konin fell silent. Before long he left the house.

Walking fast through the dark streets, he returned to the synagogue. By the light of a single candle, he looked along the shelves—shelves so stuffed with books, manuscripts, and scrolls that the very wood that held them bent and sagged.

"Here."

He pulled out a book, tattered and old. He sat down at a table and, with the light of the one candle, carefully opened the book and began to read.

What was the book? The Kabbalah. Without it, there would be no story here.

It is time to tell you about the Kabbalah.

Old it is, centuries old. Many of the pages in the book that lay before Konin were marked with symbols, diagrams, letters, and numbers in combinations that appeared nowhere else. Some believed that the Kabbalah—if used by the pious with pure heart—helped lead a soul to heaven. Others thought the book a danger, offering magic and paths not meant to be known by most men.

Konin read with such silent concentration he looked made of stone. Thereafter all of each day, hour after hour, he sat and studied the strange pages of the Kabbalah. He rose only for the required daily prayers. At night he left the synagogue. No one knew where he went or what he did. Maybe they thought a charitable Brinitzer had given him a place to sleep. But sleep he did not. What the book taught him to do, he did, and more.

You want to know what he did? You will not know. Some knowledge is not meant to be shared.

He ate nothing all week, refused all that was offered him. Except, he did not fail to accept Sender's invitations to Sabbath meals. Seeing Leah was torture to his mind and to his body, but the pain of not seeing her was greater than any other.

Came a morning when curiosity got the best of one of the other men in the synagogue. He came over to Konin and sat down beside him. "Konin," he said, "what are you doing?"

"I know what I'm doing."

"You fast from Sabbath to Sabbath."

"Believe me, it is harder to eat that one day than to fast all week long."

"But you do not study with the others, much less talk with them. It is not good to make yourself so alone. You sacrifice yourself. To what purpose? What do you want?"

Konin's voice and smile became far off, as if he dreamed. "I want a diamond. A diamond so pure its glow can fill a whole room. I want to take it to my heart, embrace it, make it mine as one with me."

"Konin, you make no sense." He shook his head. "What do you study so hard?" He bent to look.

Konin shut the book. "I told you I know what I'm doing."

But Konin's questioner had had a glimpse of the pages. "The Kabbalah," he whispered. "Konin, beware. There is danger here."

"Danger? I fear no danger."

"But you should be studying, praying—"

Konin stopped him. "Studying? Praying? Bah." He gestured toward the shelves. "All the books and all the words are dry as leaves that fall away in the cold." He pulled the Kabbalah closer. "There are other ways. Ways that live, that are alive with light and new purpose. I know what I'm doing. I know what I want and I shall have it. I learn the powers that show me the way."

Fear showed on the visitor's face. "You blaspheme. Only the purest can use the Kabbalah as you do without grave harm."

Konin put his hand on the man's arm. "I know you wish me well and want to spare me from harm. But I do not ask for much. I ask only for"—he lowered his voice—"two barrels of gold."

"Two barrels of gold? You might as well ask for a mansion in the Promised Land. What do you need such things for?"

"I need it to satisfy a man to whom gold means everything."

"In Brinitz there is only one such man. Sender."

"Yes."

"But why—" He stood and backed away. "Leah. You want Leah? But you know that Sender will never permit a poor man to marry his daughter."

"Yes."

"Konin! What are you saying?"

"I know what I say. And you see? It is working. Has Sender failed? Yes, he has failed. How many times is it now—two? Three? Four, perhaps. Each time he fails, I have won. This book—" He tapped the Kabbalah. "This book tells me how to get all—all!—that I want."

"Nothing good or holy can help you in this way."

"And if nothing good or holy, then what?"

"Konin, you frighten me. Satan awaits."

"And who created Satan? God. Therefore there is something of the holy in Satan. I am not afraid. Leave me. There is much for me to do."

The door to the synagogue banged open. "He did it! They agreed!"

All turned toward the person flying into the room.

"What?"

"Who?"

"Why so excited?"

"You'll have an attack!"

"What're you talking about?"

"Sender—" The bearer of the news stopped to catch his breath.

"Say it already. Before you drop dead from running, may I be a liar."

Breathing heavily, a hand to his chest, this is what he said. "The family agreed to Sender's terms."

"Ai, a piece of good news."

"They took long enough."

"They agreed to ten years?"

"Yes, yes. Everything!"

Sender came into the room. Smiling, patting his belly with satisfaction, he looked ready to burst with pleasure. "Jews, congratulate me."

"Mazel tov, Sender!"

"At last luck to you."

"And for Leah!"

"And the groom's family!"

"Yes," said Sender. "Ah, yes. What will be is what should be. And now, a bottle of good brandy shall be brought and all shall be joyous."

The men in the room formed a circle, arms across one another's shoulders, and began to dance and sing a wordless song in celebration.

Except for Konin.

He stood, his face as pale as paper. "No," he said. "No. It cannot be. I cannot have failed."

No one heard him, no one paid his words attention.

"For nothing," he went on. "All my sacrifices, my pain, all my study, my fasting, all the spells cast night after night—all for nothing."

His hand went to his heart. "Take my mind, take my body, take my soul. But give her to me!

"I cannot bear it. I cannot. She is destined to be mine." He held his head as if to hold back some indescribable awfulness.

Suddenly he stood stock-still.

"No. I have not failed. I have not. I know what will be. I know what fate has decreed. I have won. You hear? I have won!"

No one turned.

"I—have—won. . . ."

He fell to the floor.

At last someone noticed. "Konin, are you all right? Konin!" Patting his cheeks, splashing his face with cold water—no use.

Konin was dead.

Nu, so dead is dead. Konin was buried in the centuries-old Brinitz cemetery. Led by the Brinitzer rabbi, those gathered said the Kaddish, the prayer for the dead. Konin left no one behind to mourn or pray for him. He died as he lived—utterly alone.

Leah, barely able to stand, leaned against Fradeh for support. At last she fainted and was carried to her bed.

Dead is dead, as I said. And life continues. So plans for Leah's wedding were made. All the wealthy of Brinitz were invited. Not one but two klezmer bands played joyous music. In their fancy clothes and bedecked with jewels, the wives danced together. Their husbands, in heavy-silk black caftans and wide-brimmed hats often trimmed with fur, danced and sang in another room. For that too was the custom, that men and women even in celebration must be kept apart, as they were in the synagogue.

A rich man should share his good luck with those not so fortunate. And so the courtyard of Sender's house was filled with the poor of Brinitz, the beggars, the blind, cripples, the homeless, and the simpleminded. They too danced. When huge plates filled with food were brought out to them, they grabbed at the food and continued to dance, their mouths full, their hands and pockets stuffed with food. Who knows how long since they had eaten food not meant to be thrown away, food they had not begged or stolen. Ah, such joy. All was joy, inside the house and out.

Except for Leah. She sat with Fradeh, her face as white as the wedding dress she wore.

"Leah, why so sad? A wedding is a blessing. The groom and his family will soon be here." She patted Leah's hand. "Come, child. A little smile, would it hurt? Soon you will be united with the husband named for you in heaven. Is that not good?"

"Fradeh—"

"Yes, my Leah?"

"Where do the souls go of those who die before their time?"

"What a question!"

Dreamily, Leah went on. "What happens to the children they would have had? To the prayers they never uttered? To the thoughts they had not yet finished or had time to begin?"

"Who knows? It is not for the living to know. Dead is dead, Leah. May they rest in peace. They are gone from us."

"No, Fradeh. They are not gone. Their spirits are here, here among us."

"Leah, it is bad luck to speak of such things before a wedding. You invite evil spirits, God forbid."

"No, not evil spirits. They are not evil. They are incomplete souls. They are among us."

"Leah! What do you say?"

"I know what I say. They are among us, to complete what they could not live to do. We cannot see or hear them. But sometimes they find a way to finish what they were first born here on Earth to do."

"Oy, Leah, this is a day for happiness, not a time for such thoughts."

"My mother died when she was young. She did not complete her life. I will go to the cemetery and ask her spirit to come to my wedding, as she would had she lived. She will be near me under the canopy, just as my father will."

"You are not afraid?"

"Dear Fradeh, of what should I be afraid?"

Fradeh sighed deeply. "All right, child. I will come with you."

"No. I must go alone."

"Then I will wait outside the gates."

Leah nodded, and together they rose.

"Fradeh," Leah asked as they walked, "is it allowed to ask other spirits to come to my wedding?"

Fradeh shook her head firmly. "No, child. Only the closest blood relatives. To awaken other spirits is sinful. Why do you ask?"

Leah did not answer.

They arrived at the cemetery gates. Fradeh waited there, and Leah entered the graveyard alone.

The cemetery was filled with tombstones, one right after the other. Some so old they leaned against another, others worn smooth by who knows how many years. Whatever spirits lurked there remained silent and still.

Leah knew where her mother's grave lay. But that is not what she looked for. Quickly she moved among the stones, looking this way and that. And for what?

Konin's grave.

She found it. On her knees, she put her arms around the stone.

"Konin, my love." She wept. "Beloved. You have always been my beloved, even before I knew you.

"Oh, how I want you with me. Without you all is dark, bare, without life. I live like a golem.

"You come to my dreams every night, dearest one. Shall we be together no other way? No more than that? It is not enough, not enough.

"You were taken too soon, my Konin. We did not have the life together we were meant to have, nor the children to bless our lives. We did not complete what we were meant to finish, each with the other." She rested her cheek against the cold stone.

"Last night—" Her trembling fingers stroked the letters of his name. "Last night I dreamed you asked me to invite you to my wedding.

"And if I do? What then? Is this forbidden? It cannot be. Where I am, there you must be too. Surely, surely, I can be forgiven my yearning for you." She grasped the stone between her two hands.

"I do not know what will be, but whatever will be, will be."

She drew a deep breath and spoke.

"Konin, come to my wedding!"

In the courtyard, Sender was wringing his hands with worry. "Where is the bridegroom and his family? Soon they'll be late. God forbid something should have happened to them. Go—" He nodded toward a young boy. "Go, run along the path in their direction. Maybe you'll see something. Go."

The boy ran off, but soon he came back. "They're coming! I can see the wagon."

"Thanks be."

With a great clatter of wheels and horse's hooves, a wagon pulled into the courtyard. Out stepped the groom's father and several guests. A second wagon brought the groom and yet more guests.

Sender embraced the groom's father. "Nachman, welcome! Sholem aleichim. The trip was all right?"

"Oy, what a journey. Aleichim sholem. First a mistake and we went the wrong way. Then we almost were swallowed alive by a swamp. Wolves howled at us as we went. I myself began to think of evil omens, may my mouth be cleansed. But you see, here we are, and yet in time."

"And the groom?" Sender opened his arms. "Ah, sholem aleichim, Menashe! Blessed is the day you are here." He kissed the young man on both cheeks.

Well, what was he like, this young man from a wealthy family and, the family said, with a mind of brilliance and learning? He was not beautiful, let me tell you.

Menashe was short. His sparse sidelocks showed his hair to be light brown. He was narrow and thin, a flea of a man. Very nervous, frightened maybe, so when he spoke in his high voice, he stuttered.

"A-a-a-aleichim sh-sh-sh-sholem, R-R-Reb S-S-Sen-Sen-Sender. A-a-a g-great d-d-d-day."

Sender spoke. "Come. Go into the house. Eat, freshen up a little, rest a moment after the long trip."

"Oy, what a pleasure, Sender." Nachman sighed. "But we have little time, so only for a moment."

"Then only for a moment. But come, come." Sender led the groom's wedding party into the house.

Fradeh appeared, her arm around Leah's waist as if to hold her up. Leah seemed barely able to walk.

"Leah, Fradeh—where have you been?"

"The bride's dress is wrinkled!"

"And dirty."

"So how come?"

"What was so important it couldn't wait?"

"We were getting worried—bad luck before a wedding."

"What happened?"

Fradeh shook her head. "Do not ask what happened. I myself am not sure. I know little, understand less. She fainted. I could not wake her—I even thought she might be dead."

"Oy, terrible, terrible."

"Now," Fradeh went on, "I am afraid something dreadful will happen, may God prove me wrong. There are evil spirits everywhere."

"Bite your tongue! To mention them is to invite them."

"Ai, foolishness. Enough already!"

"Enough already is right. Leah must be made ready."

Leah was brought into the house. The wrinkles in her dress were smoothed out as much as hands alone could do it, and the dirt removed with a damp cloth. Through all that happened, she barely spoke. Her eyes seemed to look inward, seeing things that others could not know.

Leah was brought out into the courtyard. Seated, she was to wait for the bridegroom.

Menashe approached, the bridal veil in his hands. The hands trembled a little, but he managed to put the veil over the bride's head and pull it down over her face.

Leah bolted into the present. She tore the veil from her face, pushed Menashe away. "You are not my bridegroom!"

The crowded courtyard fell into shocked silence.

Sender, shaking, went over to her. "Leah! My daughter! What are you doing? What do you mean?"

She shoved him aside.

Wild-eyed, she looked around. And then she spoke in a loud voice.

"Ah! I wear death's shroud and lie under the earth. But I have returned to my destined bride. Now she is mine. I will be with her forever. Never will I leave her!"

The voice was not her own. It was strong, deep, a man's voice.

Sender tried to touch her. "My angel, loved light of my life, Leah—"

"Murderer!" she shouted at him.

Sender backed away. "She has gone mad."

The rabbi, present through all, spoke softly. "Ai, Jews of Brinitz. She is not mad." He shook his head.

"A dybbuk has entered the body of the bride."

Part II

So what is a dybbuk, you may well ask? It is the soul of one who has died. But the soul can find no peace, either because of some great sin, or because something important to the heavens was left undone in its lifetime on Earth. It is tortured by demons, moves endlessly in pain, searching always for rest and comfort. Sometimes it will enter the body of a living person. The person it chooses may also have sinned, and in sinning has left an opening for the wandering soul to enter. There at last the soul can find a resting place.

So it was here. Konin's sin was his calling on Satan, black is the name, and through his use of the Kabbalah for reasons that were without virtue and impure. And Leah's sin? To ask Konin's spirit to her wedding. That is forbidden. It is possible to love too much. But then, who is to say what is too much?

The rabbi's words ended the silence in the courtyard. The crowd, all talking at once, backed away from what they had seen and heard. In their homes, in the marketplace, in the synagogue, what else could be the topic of conversation?

"A dybbuk. Oy."

"Never before in Brinitz."

"Luck like this we needed?"

"What does it have to do with us? Leah—"

"Nu, what about Leah? What did she—"

"Yes, what did she do to deserve a dybbuk?"

"Ai, no one deserves a dybbuk."

"They don't come out of nowhere!"

"For no reason!"

"True, true. But—"

"Who are we to know? Sender—"

"Sender suffers too."

"He only wanted the best."

"The best! Who knows what is the best?"

"The Almighty knows."

"He makes no mistakes!"

"So the mistake was Sender's?"

"Do I know?"

"So what is to be done?"

"I hear—"

"What can you hear that we don't already know?"

"I hear," the speaker repeated, "that in Miropol there is—"

"Yes! The great Rabbi of Miropol. The wisest of the wise."

"Ah. Rabbi Azriel. A tsaddik—a miracle worker. They say—"

"They say he knows everything. One word from him is like a gold coin from heaven."

"So?"

"Do we know what to do with"—he shuddered—"with a dybbuk?"

"No, we do not. Rabbi Azriel—"

"Yes, yes. Rabbi Azriel, he maybe will know."

"Maybe? Not maybe. He will know."

"Sender should go to him with Leah."

"So what is Sender waiting for?"

"Who knows? Who can understand what a father feels when such a thing happens?"

"He will know. Rabbi Azriel's goodness and power are talked of everywhere."

"I hear—"

"What did you hear?"

"I hear that he leaves tomorrow, that—"

"Who leaves tomorrow?"

"Sender, who else."

"You couldn't say this right away?"

"Right away, not right away! Sender leaves with Leah and Fradeh and goes to Miropol tomorrow."

"Oy, what will happen?"

"Who knows?"

"We shall see, we shall see. . . ."

Rabbi Azriel of Miropol sat alone in his study. As usual, a book lay open before him. He was very old. Wrinkles and deep lines marked his face. They came not only from age, but also from his knowledge of the pains and sorrows of Jews everywhere—and not only of Jews. He understood the world too well.

Mikel, his assistant and almost as old as he, came to him and spoke softly. "Rabbi."

Kissing the page, the rabbi closed the book. "Yes."

"Rabbi, there is a visitor to see you. Reb Sender—"

"—from Brinitz, I know."

"His daughter, an only child, is—"

"—possessed by a dybbuk. I know."

"So shall I—"

"Tell him to come in. Him alone."

Sender came into the room, his arms outstretched. "Rabbi! Help me! Save my child!"

"How did this terrible thing happen?"

"As I remember, just as the bridegroom—"

"That's not what I'm asking. He could not have entered without cause. What has she done to permit this?"

"My daughter is all virtue and God-fearing, a goodness that—"

"Has anyone asked the dybbuk who he is?"

"Rabbi, we know who he is. We recognized his voice. He is Konin. A poor scholar who came to Brinitz from who knows where. He ate often at my table."

"And?"

"He died suddenly a few months ago. They say he became impure because he used the Kabbalah for selfish reasons."

"And?"

"He wanted two barrels of gold."

"And?"

"He said there was holiness in Satan, curse the name, because God created Satan. Oy, Rabbi, help me!"

"Sender," he said, "did anyone ask him why he attached himself to your daughter?"

"Yes, Rabbi, but he would not answer."

"When he was a guest in your house, did you mistreat him? Embarrass him? Did you in any way offend him?"

"Rabbi, I have searched my mind over and over. Gladly I would do penance for anything hurtful or wrong. But I cannot remember that I did. I am only human!"

"Memory is faulty."

"But Rabbi, why attach himself to my daughter? Why?"

"Sometimes children are punished for the sins of the parents."

"But—but—I cannot think of anything . . ."

"Send in the girl."

Sender opened the door. Fradeh and Leah rose from their seats. As they got to the door, Leah stopped.

"Leah, the rabbi asked for you," Sender said. "My dove, come into the room. Come."

Leah did not move. "I—I—I want to. But I cannot."

"Maiden, come in," said Rabbi Azriel.

Leah walked slowly toward the rabbi.

"Sit down," he said.

She sat. Suddenly she jumped up and spoke in the voice not her own.

"No! I don't want to! Let me be!" She tried to run out of the room but was stopped by Fradeh and Sender.

Rabbi Azriel's voice was firm and strong. "Dybbuk, tell us who you are."

"Rabbi of Miropol, you know who I am."

"I am not asking for your name. I am asking what in life brought you here."

"I am one who sought different paths."

"Only those who wander from the straight path seek different ones."

"That path is too narrow."

The rabbi sighed deeply and shook his head. "Why did you enter the body of Leah?"

"I alone am to be her bridegroom. It is to be no other. It is so destined."

"The dead are forbidden to dwell among the living."

"I am not dead."

"You have departed this world. You are not to return until the End of Days. Therefore I now command you to leave the body of this living maiden."

"Rabbi of Miropol!" the dybbuk shouted. **"I know how strong you are. I know you can control the angels themselves. But you cannot control me. I will not leave."**

The dybbuk's voice shook. **"I have nowhere to go. All paths are closed to me. I am pursued by demons and evil spirits. They torture me. Endless agony and wandering are all that I know. There is Earth, and there is heaven,**

and there are endless universes in heaven. But none will allow me entrance to find peace.

"Rabbi of Miropol! Have pity! Now that I have found a place of rest, a place without pain, I will not leave. You cannot make me leave."

"I am filled with deepest pity and sorrow for you, wandering soul," the rabbi said. "I will use all my powers to free you from the evil ones that torture you. That I swear. But you must leave the body of this maiden."

"I will not!"

"Dybbuk, if you do not leave her at my words, then I will be forced to sever you from all Jews living and dead and from the Holy Torah. You will be excommunicated, banished eternally."

"Oh, Rabbi of Miropol! I am not afraid of what you can do. You will cut me off from the world of Jews here and in other worlds? And from the Torah? You will banish me?" The dybbuk laughed. "There is no pain worse than the pain I have known and will know, no loneliness greater, if I lose the haven I have found. I am not afraid of all your words and all your threats." He screamed. "I will not leave my destined bride! She is mine for-ever!"

At that Leah's eyes closed and she slumped in her chair. She awoke, then, as herself. "What happened? Where—where am I?"

"Shhh, my child," said Fradeh, "all is well. The rabbi did not hurt you. Calm, calm."

The rabbi put his hands over his eyes. For a few moments all was silent. Then he spoke.

"Sender, all of you—leave me. Send in Mikel."

Mikel arrived. "Your wish, Rabbi?"

"An excommunication cannot take place without the agreement of the chief rabbi of the community. Go to Rabbi Shimson and tell him I need to see him about a most important matter."

It did not take long for Rabbi Shimson to arrive.

Rabbi Azriel explained—about Leah and the dybbuk, and who the dybbuk was, that he refused to leave. "So therefore, Rabbi Shimson, I must expel him by exorcism, and request your permission then to perform an excommunication."

"Ai, it is terrible enough for a living person, how much worse for the dead. There is no other way?"

"No, there is not."

"Well then, so be it. Did the dybbuk explain why he claimed the girl?"

"No, he did not."

Rabbi Shimson paused before he spoke. "Reb Azriel, it may be that what I am about to tell you will help in some way, I know not how."

"Ah, yes? Let me hear."

"Last night I had a dream—three times I had the same, identical dream."

"The dream may not be ignored."

"Do you remember a Nisson ben Rivke? He came to you many times when he was a student."

"Yes, I remember. I heard he died while yet a young man."

"It was he in my dream. Three times he came, and three times he demanded that Sender of Brinitz appear before a rabbinical court in his name."

"What can be his claim against Sender?"

"That I do not know. Not fully."

"But some you do know."

"Yes. I did not understand all, but a little. There was something about a pact between him and Sender that Sender had broken."

"Well, the demand must be obeyed. But what has this to do with the dybbuk?"

"He said that his son, Konin, was taken from life before his preordained end because of that broken pact."

"Ah."

"The maiden is Sender's daughter, so . . ."

"Yes. There may be the connection."

Sender was told to come in.

"Reb Sender, do you remember Nisson ben Rivke?"

"Nisson?" His eyes opened wide. "Yes, I remember, Rabbi. He was the friend of my heart through childhood and when we were young men."

"And?"

"He left Brinitz. I heard no more of him."

"And?"

"Rabbi, Rabbi, what do you want from me?"

"No, Sender. That is not the question. Think, Sender, think. Nisson ben Rivke's spirit has demanded—through Reb Shimson—that you appear before a rabbinical court for judgment."

"Me? What—what could I have done?"

"Think, Sender, think."

"Rabbi, I tear through my memory and can find nothing, nothing."

"Think again, Sender. The dead make no demand without good reason. Where have you failed?"

The room filled with silence as Sender closed his eyes and lowered his head. Then he spoke, his voice shadowed by tears.

"Rabbi, I remember. Forgive me! I had forgotten!"

"It is not for me to forgive you. What do you remember?"

"Nisson and I—we—we made a pact that if his wife gave birth to a son and mine to a daughter, they would—they would marry."

"And?"

"Ai! Konin! Konin was his son. I felt something. I did, I was drawn to him. But how could I have known he was Nisson's son?"

"You could have known had you willed it so."

"But Rabbi, how could I give my Leah to him? How? He had no home, he

43

wandered from place to place, ate crusts of bread, lived from the charity of others."

"So?"

"She would have lived with hunger and in rags."

"You are not poor, Sender."

"Oy, Rabbi, forgive me, forgive me!" Sender cried. "I meant no harm, I did not want to disturb the heavens, God forbid. Nor the spirit of my loved friend. Forgive me!"

"It is not up to me," said the Rabbi. "Sender, where are the bridegroom and his family?"

"They remain in my house until after the Sabbath."

"Direct the fastest rider to go to them and tell them to come here as soon as possible."

"Yes, Rabbi. But why—"

Rabbi Azriel stopped him. "Leave me now. I will call for you when you are needed here. The rabbinical court will by then be assembled."

Rabbi Azriel called Mikel.

"Mikel, the spirit of Nisson ben Rivke must be asked to be present during a rabbinical court. Do not tremble, Mikel. There is nothing to fear. Put up a curtain and cover the eastern wall. Behind the curtain is where he will be and remain."

It was done.

"Now, Mikel, listen to me carefully."

"Yes, Rabbi."

"Take my cane. Go to the cemetery. With my cane to guide you, enter with your eyes closed. When my cane stops you at a tombstone, rap on it three times. Then say:

"'Spirits of the dead, forgive my disturbing you. But the soul of one among you is needed here on Earth. Nisson ben Rivke! The great Rabbi of Miropol, blessed be he, summons you to him. The rabbinical court you demand will meet with you and Sender of Brinitz. The injustice done to you will be redeemed, God willing. Come.'

"Then, Mikel, turn away and leave. Pay no attention, do not turn back, do not look, no matter how loud or terrible are the shrieks and cries of the spirits you have awakened. Do you understand?"

"I understand." Mikel left, the rabbi's cane in his hand.

"Reb Shimson, in respect of your knowledge and station, stay and be a member of the rabbinical council. I ask further that you learn from Nisson ben Rivke's disturbed spirit the nature of his complaint against Sender."

"May I be granted such wisdom in truth. I will stay and do what you ask."

"Also, I would like you to conduct the wedding ceremony when it is time."

"The wedding ceremony . . . I accept what you say and concede to your greater knowledge, Reb Azriel. In light of that knowledge and your great virtue, you will carry out the exorcism and excommunication if the dybbuk yet refuses to leave."

"I will."

Rabbi Azriel summoned other rabbis to serve as judges on the court, telling them to bring their prayer shawls and phylacteries, called tefillin. When they arrived, he explained. When they expressed fear, he calmed them.

Mikel returned. "It is done."

"Call in Sender."

Sender, pale and frightened, came silently into the room.

"Has the wedding party arrived?" Rabbi Azriel asked.

"No, it has not."

"Mikel, send the swiftest messenger and tell them to hurry. Sender."

"Yes, Rabbi." His voice shook.

"Sender, we have sent word to Nisson ben Rivke, pure now in death, that the rabbinical court calls him to a trial with you. Will you accept the court's verdict?"

45

"I will."

"Will you carry out what the court directs?"

"I will."

Rabbi Azriel turned toward the curtain.

"Pure deceased Nisson ben Rivke, we have assembled this rabbinical court to hear your claim against Sender of Brinitz. We do this in fear and righteousness according to the Law, at your behest. You will remain invisible to us where you are at this moment, and only those who must hear will hear."

All in the room waited in silence for what was to come.

The curtain on the eastern wall moved as though a breeze had brushed it.

"He has come," whispered one of the men.

"Yes, he has come," said the other.

"We begin," said the rabbi. The men placed the tefillin on their left arms and forehead, pulled their prayer shawls over their heads and covered their faces, and faced the eastern wall.

Reb Shimson addressed the spirit. "Pure spirit of Nisson ben Rivke, we apologize for disturbing your rest."

The curtain moved slightly.

"From the World to Come that we here do not yet know, you have told of a claim against Sender of Brinitz. The rabbinical court is assembled in answer to your request."

Again the curtain moved.

"We ask, in the name of the Almighty, Blessed Be He, that you grant us the knowledge of your claim, so that we may render true and honest judgment."

"I hear sound but no words," whispered one rabbi.

"I hear words but no sound," said another.

Reb Shimson addressed Sender. "Sender of Brinitz, the pure deceased Nisson ben Rivke states that in your youth you and he were loved friends."

"That is true," said Sender.

"He states further that you and he made a pact during the High Holy Days. You swore that when you each married, if the Master of the World granted a son to one and a daughter to the other, they would marry."

"That is true."

"The son was Konin, whom you came to know. When Nisson ben Rivke passed from this world, he saw that his son wandered in loneliness, searching for he knew not what. The pure deceased says that his son searched without knowing for his predestined bride, your daughter, Leah."

"I have learned so."

"The pure deceased states that you saw that they loved each other, but his son was poor. So you closed your eyes and memory and broke the pact between you. He explains that you sought wealth alone for your daughter."

"That is so."

"Nisson ben Rivke has said that his son called upon the Evil One so that he could, living, have your daughter as his bride."

"I have heard so."

"In this he failed."

"Yes."

"The spirit states that his son died when you betrothed your daughter to another."

"Yes."

"Because of Konin's sin, his calling upon the Dark One, his soul has wandered homeless since then and in pain none living can know."

"Yes."

"The pure deceased says more, that your daughter asked his son's spirit to her wedding. He came to her wedding, so that he could possess your daughter not as the heavens meant, but that allowed the two to become one. The pact between you and the deceased had so decreed, yet not in this way. He lives in her body and speaks through her mouth."

"Yes."

"Because you broke the pact between you, and Konin was his only child, he remains alone in the World to Come with no heirs to his name on this Earth, therefore with no one to remember and mourn for him with the Kaddish."

"Yes."

Rabbi Azriel stood and conferred quietly with those in the room. He turned toward the eastern wall. "Pure spirit," he said, "we have heard your claim and render this judgment."

He faced Sender, who stood frozen. "Sender of Brinitz, we have heard the claim of Nisson ben Rivke and agree that you broke the pledge between you that had been accepted in the heavens as binding forever. Hear our verdict."

Sender lowered his head.

"You will give half your wealth to the poor."

"I will."

"Further, for as long as you live, you will say the Kaddish and mourn each year for Nisson ben Rivke and his son, Konin, so that their memories may live, just as you would for those of your own family."

"I will."

Facing the eastern wall again, Rabbi Azriel said: "Nisson ben Rivke! You have heard our verdict and the acceptance of Sender of Brinitz. Do you accept our verdict as well? Will you forgive the loved friend of your youth?"

There was a moment's silence. The curtain did not move.

"This court now pleads with you as the father of Konin to tell your son to leave the body of the maiden Leah. In return, the Almighty will shine His grace and goodness upon you and your lost son."

All in the room said, "Amen." Again, the curtain lay still.

"Pure dead, the trial between you and Sender of Brinitz is now at an end. Return to your eternal rest, harming nothing living as you go." The curtain lay flat against the wall.

"Mikel, take down the curtain. Bring water."

The curtain was removed, the men took off their prayer shawls and removed the tefillin, and Mikel brought in a basin and pitcher of water. All present poured water over their hands, so that they would be cleansed of any trace of the dead.

Reb Shimson spoke softly to the rabbis. "Did you notice that the spirit did not say he accepted the verdict?"

They nodded.

"Did you notice that he did not say he forgave Sender?"

They nodded.

"Did you notice that he did not say 'Amen'?"

They nodded.

"Ai!" cried Reb Shimson. "Bad omens all."

"We are no longer needed here." The other rabbis left the room.

"Mikel," said Rabbi Azriel, "has the bridegroom's party arrived?"

"I have not heard their horses, Rabbi."

"Send the swiftest messenger and tell them to rush here, to fly! In the meantime, have the wedding canopy set up and the musicians told to get ready. The daughter Leah should dress in her wedding gown. Reb Shimson, please remain."

"Yes, Rabbi."

Mikel did as he was told and returned.

"Let the maiden be brought."

Leah entered, wearing her wedding gown. A long black cloak lay over her shoulders. Her face was without color, her eyes blank as one in a trance. Slowly she sat down facing the rabbi.

"Dybbuk, in the name of the chief rabbi of Miropol who here sits beside me, in the name of the holy community of Jews living and dead, in the name of the great judges of ancient Israel, I command you to leave the body of Leah."

"I will not!"

"Mikel, call in men to witness what will come."

Forgive me, Dear Reader. I cannot explain the meaning of all that happened and all that was spoken in that room. I am, after all, only a poor writer—and, some would say, a poor Jew as well. I will tell what I can of what was said and done and what, at last, happened. It is the best I can do.

Fourteen men came in, each carrying a white shroud. Seven were given hollowed-out ram's horns, the seven others handed Torah scrolls. Seven black candles were brought into the room.

"Dybbuk!" said Rabbi Azriel. "In the name of Israel I commit you to the first level of spirits, who will rip you out with all their strength. Sound the horns!"

The horns sounded a long single note.

Leah rocked back and forth in her chair. "Eeeee!" screamed the dybbuk's voice. "I will not leave! I cannot go!"

"Dybbuk! If you will not leave, I commit you to the second level of spirits. Sound the horns!"

The horns sounded three short notes.

Leah rose from her chair, thrashing, her body twisting from side to side. "Let me be! I will not let go! No, no, no!"

Leah fell back into the chair. Her hands as fists beat on the chair's arms. "Ohh, ohh, ohh!" groaned the dybbuk. "The pain, the pain. All the powers are against me now. My father too! Demons and evil spirits tear at me—the agony, the agony! There is no mercy. Oh, the pain, the terrible unnameable pain!"

Leah sat upright. "But I will not depart. I will not." Yet the voice was softer than before. "Whatever strength stays within me will make it so. I will remain."

"Mikel," said the rabbi, "return the scrolls to their place. Cover the Ark with a black cloth. Light the black candles. All here put on the white shroud." His arms upraised, Rabbi Azriel spoke in a thunderous voice.

"Oh Lord, rise up! Let all thine enemies fall away like lifeless leaves! Oh, thou stubborn spirit, in the name of the Almighty I rip from you all ties that connect you with this Earth and the living! I tear asunder all ties that bind you to all of Israel and to all that is holy to Jews. I banish you, I excommunicate you. Sound the horns!"

The horns sounded a series of short notes.

"Oh, oh, my strength is leaving me." Leah slumped in her chair. **"I am weak, so weak, weak. . . ."**

"I command that you leave the living body of the maiden Leah!"

"Woe. Oh, woe. I am losing, I am losing. . . . Where shall I go, what shall I do?"

"Do you swear to leave the maiden's living body and never return?"

"I swear." The voice was a whisper.

Rabbi Azriel spoke again, his tone fervent in prayer. "Almighty God, by the same power that allowed me to cast out this spirit, I hereby revoke the cutting off from all Israel. Allow this for the sake of the virtue that held special place in the living Konin before its corruption, for the sake of the pure dead his father Nisson ben Rivke, for the sake of the merits of his ancestors. Permit this in the name of your infinite compassion and eternal justice."

The dybbuk spoke in a trembling voice. **"I am finished. I am dying. Say the Kaddish for me."**

"Sender, recite the Kaddish."

Sender recited the ancient prayer, which begins *"Yisgadal v'Yiskadash sh'me rabbo . . .,"* which means "Magnified and sanctified be the great name of God. . . ."

Leah jumped up. **"Ah—ah—ah . . ."** She collapsed into the chair.

The door blew hard open, and then slammed shut as if by a sudden harsh wind.

"The dybbuk is gone." Rabbi Azriel sat down and put his head in his hands. The hands trembled.

"Mikel," he said, "collect the black candles, remove the black cloth from the Torah, and all others leave now. Take the white shrouds with you. Fradeh will remain with the maiden. The groom's family, Mikel—where are they?"

"I will see, Rabbi."

Fradeh came and sat in a chair beside Leah.

Mikel followed close behind her. "Rabbi!" he said. "A wheel broke on their wagon. They walked the rest of the way. But they are near—they have been seen."

"More delay. Ai, what is happening here? We must go to meet them. But first—" He took his cane and marked a circle around Leah's chair. The circle seemed made of flames that quickly died and left no mark. "We must hurry!" He left the room.

Fradeh took Leah's hand. In a moment the girl's eyes opened and she awoke.

"Where am I?" She looked around the room. "What has happened?"

Fradeh patted her hand and spoke softly. "Nothing has happened but good things, my Leah."

"I feel so empty."

"Believe me, in a little while you will be filled with happiness. Your bridegroom comes; the wedding canopy awaits. Relax a little, child. I will sing you a lullaby."

Fradeh began to sing a lullaby from Leah's childhood. "*Ai lilla-looleh, so schloff mein kind . . .*" Fradeh herself fell asleep.

Leah did not. She closed her eyes and sighed deeply. Another sigh seemed to answer her.

Her eyes opened. "Who sighed with such sadness?"

"I did."

"Where are you?"

"I am here with you."

"I can't see you."

"I am not permitted to be seen."

"Who are you?"

"I don't remember. Only if you can remember, can I."

"Your voice. It is known to me."

"Yes."

"How? Where?" She paused. "Oh! I remember!"

"Yes."

"Can it truly be?"

"As it must be."

"Konin!" she cried. "My loved one, Konin."

"Yes."

"Oh, you with the soft hair, with eyes that shone, with a voice like music. You, who filled my dreams every night, whose touch I never knew. You, whom I loved with a yearning almost not of this world. Why did you leave me?"

"Living, I left you. By man's measure, dead I returned to live again through you. But I was not allowed to remain. I fought the unseen powers of heaven and of Earth to remain, but they would not allow me to stay. I was expelled from you, and from this Earth."

"Justice, where is justice and where is mercy? We have been forever destined to be together. Why must we be apart? Why can we not ever know the happiness of other mortals? Why can we not ever have the joy of becoming as one? Why can we not ever have the blessings of children to love us as we would love them?"

The sound of wedding music came into the room from the outside.

"Konin, they are coming for me. They will marry me to a stranger."

She stood. The black cloak fell from her shoulders. "Konin, come to me!"

"I cannot. A circle around you holds me back."

"Then I will come to you." With one step, she moved outside the realm of the circle.

The figure of Konin appeared, dressed in white as a bridegroom.

"Ah," she cried with joy. "The barrier between us is no more."

"You are free now, beloved."

"I am coming to you, my bridegroom."

"Come to me, my bride."

"I am coming to you."

"I am coming to you."

"Never apart, never again apart."

"I have left your body and enter your soul."

The two figures merged as one.

Konin's spirit vanished. Leah's lifeless body slid to the floor.

The door opened.

Rabbi Azriel entered and stopped. "It is too late."

"Leah! My daughter!" Sender sobbed.

"My little bird!" Fradeh cried out.

"What has been was decreed," said the rabbi. "What has been is what must be. I will argue with the Almighty another day."

I have told this story in my own way. Some say it could not have happened, but I think it could have. There are those who think it is a sad tale, meant to frighten young and old and to teach them a lesson. Exactly what that lesson is, I'm not sure about myself. Are you?

AUTHOR'S NOTE

The idea of a dybbuk is very old, even when it is not called by that name. Simply put, the personality, spirit, or soul of someone who has died enters the body of someone who is alive. The behavior of the living person changes and becomes strange, or like the person whose spirit has taken over. The idea exists in almost all cultures throughout the world, either believed as true or accepted as superstition. It is just about universal.

For centuries, Jews called the spirit who took control of a living person a "dybbuk." Some extremely religious Jews believe in the possibility of possession by a dybbuk to this day.

The story as told here is very roughly based on a play by S. Ansky (1863–1920) called *The Dybbuk: Between Two Worlds*. It was first produced in 1920. Written in Russian, the play has been translated and performed worldwide since then. It has been the basis for movies, for operas and other music, for poetry, even for painting and sculpture.

I have stripped down the play's plot to a basic core and added some elements that do not appear in the original. The result is a story that stands on its own. It is, after all, a kind of love story. A strange love story, yes. About a love that defies custom, reason, religion, perhaps even the divine. Leah and Konin were meant to be together. Nothing could be allowed to change that, not even death itself. It's as simple as that.

A note about arranged marriages. They are the rule, not the exception, in several cultures—especially outside the Western world. They were the rule among religious Jews during the period of the story and remain not uncommon among certain kinds of Jews today. In the extreme, neither bride nor groom could see each other before the wedding ceremony. My maternal grandfather and grandmother's marriage was an arranged one. They had never seen each other. But my grandfather broke the rules—he sneaked a look at my grandmother before the wedding day. "Ah, she was so beautiful, I fell in love with her on the spot!" Or so he told us.

On an even more personal note, the lullaby that Fradeh sings to Leah on page 55 was sung to me as a child. It is soothing, calming, a sure route to sleep or to the relief of pain or illness. I didn't know what most of the words meant then, and I still don't know.

Allow me to continue with the personal. I am a Jew, yes. But not a religious or practicing one. Most of what I have learned has come from much research and endless conversation. My family origins are in Eastern Europe. There lay the center of the Jewish world, a rich and vibrant life extinguished forever by the murders of the Nazi Holocaust. So although the particulars of the religious practices had to be learned late by me as an adult, that world remains precious to me as a reflection of the past. Writing about it is a token of gratitude and remembrance of my heritage. It is also a warm reflection of my parents and a loving tribute to them.

The Judaism described here is of a special kind. The Brinitz townspeople were not only extremely religious. They were Chassids, sometimes spelled Hassids. Many of the customs and much of the behavior are common to all religious Jews. But Chassidism is different in some basic ways. Founded by Rabbi Israel Baal Shem Tov (1698–1760), it changed the emphasis on the learning of the Talmud and Torah for their own sakes, and emphasized instead the goodness and compassion of a merciful God. His presence could be expressed through nature and the everyday. It became possible for anyone to be a "good Jew," as long as he behaved ethically and with kindness toward his fellow man and all living things. The singing and dancing in the story are characteristic of such Jews. Joy and laughter formed major parts of the Chassidic life. God was good and life was good, even when life was miserable. After all, being alive was a gift from God, so how could it be anything but good? Maybe sad, hard, poor, painful, but being alive was itself a reason for celebration and gratitude. In fact, there is nothing in all of nature that is not cause for joy, for all of nature is created by God just as humans have been.

Dybbuk is as accurate as I could make it. Some things are simplified, some terms and concepts altered to be more easily understood by a modern, nonreligious Jew or non-Jewish reader. In other words, any mistakes or grievous religious errors are my responsibility alone.

But all this is background and a kind of explanation. What about the story you hold in your hands? It tells itself. There is no more to say about it than that.

DEFINITIONS

ALEICHIM SHOLEM: (*See* Sholem aleichim)

The EASTERN WALL: (*See* The Promised Land) Israel is to the east of Europe and America. The most important prayers are recited facing that wall, and critical events are conducted facing the same direction. To have a synagogue seat along the eastern wall was and is considered to be a mark of a man's importance or piety.

GOLEM: A being resembling a human but who is not complete. Traditionally a golem cannot speak and cannot think for himself. He is often thought to be made of clay, magically brought to life by a tsaddik. The Frankenstein monster is a kind of golem.

HIGH HOLY DAYS: The ten days that mark the beginning of the Jewish New Year and could be said to be the birthday of the world. Although a period of repentance and prayer, these days are spent with family and friends and are a time of happiness. These are days of God's judgment of men. The judgment is sealed for the coming year on Yom Kippur, the last day, the most solemn and holy of all religious holidays.

HOLLOWED-OUT RAM'S HORN: Called the *shofar*. Ten to twelve inches long, it is blown in the synagogue only on the highest of religious holidays, such as the start of the New Year (Rosh Hashana) and Yom Kippur (Day of Repentance and Atonement). Otherwise it may be blown only under exceptional circumstances, as here with the exorcism of the dybbuk.

KABBALAH: A collection of writings and teachings that are believed to help connect humans with the mysteries of creation and life, and possibly even to offer ways to God.

It arose as a force within Judaism in the thirteenth century, but it is thought to have first appeared as early as the eighth century. It was added to by later scholars and mystics. The Kabbalah is complex, mysterious, and very difficult to understand. The text offers symbols and rituals not found elsewhere, some of them with magical possibilities.

KADDISH: The mourner's prayer. It contains no reference to death. Essentially it is a glorification of God and is an expression of faith.

KLEZMER: A small group of musicians that traveled from town to town, playing folk songs and traditional dances at weddings and other celebrations.

MAZEL TOV: Congratulations!

The PROMISED LAND: Israel. Originally the Jewish homeland, Jews were forced to leave because of persecution by the pharaohs in ancient Egypt, eventually scattering worldwide. It is believed to be promised to the Jews as their homeland by God.

REB: The equivalent of "mister."

SHOLEM ALEICHIM: The traditional greeting of Jews, a kind of hello. It means "peace unto you." The immediate and expected reply is "Aleichim Sholem," a reversal of the words, which means the same thing.

TALMUD: A collection of more than 60 books that are commentaries on the Torah (*see definition*). It interprets the Torah, and defines the rules and laws that affect all aspects of Jewish life. It deals with rules of behavior in daily and religious life, ranging from diet and economics, dress and medicine, ethics and sexuality, astronomy and mathematics—topics that touch the life of all humans, especially Jews. It is studied intensely and argued about endlessly among the pious.

TEFILLIN: Also called phylacteries. Two small square leather boxes containing biblical passages. They are placed on the left arm and forehead, held in place by thin leather straps. They are to be worn during weekday morning prayers and in other exceptional circumstances.

TORAH: The first five books of the Bible: Genesis, Exodus, Leviticus, Numbers, Deuteronomy. They are the central sacred scriptures of Judaism.

TSADDIK: An extremely pious person, considered holy. Sometimes believed to be in touch with the supernatural and able to perform magic.